## Construction Zone

# Demolition

by JoAnn Early Macken

**Consulting Editor:** Gail Saunders-Smith, PhD

**Consultant:** Don Matson, owner
Metro Construction, Paving, and Excavating
Roseville, Minnesota

Capstone press®

Mankato, Minnesota

Pebble Plus is published by Capstone Press,
151 Good Counsel Drive, P.O. Box 669, Mankato, Minnesota 56002.
www.capstonepress.com

1  2  3  4  5  6  13  12  11  10  09  08

*Library of Congress Cataloging-in-Publication Data*
Macken, JoAnn Early, 1953–
    Demolition/by JoAnn Early Macken.
    p. cm. — (Pebble plus. Construction zone)
    Summary: "Simple text and photographs present building demolition, including information on the
workers and equipment needed"— Provided by publisher.
    Includes bibliographical references and index.
    ISBN-13: 978-1-4296-1237-1 (hardcover)
    ISBN-10: 1-4296-1237-1 (hardcover)
    1. Wrecking — Juvenile literature.  I. Title. II. Series.
TH447.M33 2008
690'.26 — dc22                                                    2007027114

**Editorial Credits**
Sarah L. Schuette, editor; Patrick Dentinger, designer; Jo Miller, photo researcher

**Photo Credits**
Alamy/Michael Doolittle, 19
Corbis/Reuters/Mohamed Azakir, cover
Dreamstime/Mitar Holod, 13; Tomas Hajek, 9
iStockphoto/Bryan Lever, 15
Shutterstock/Alexey Fateev, 1; David Wayne Deveney, 11; Mark William Richardson; 5;
    Milos Jokic, 17; oksanaperkins, 21
SuperStock Inc./Raymond Forbes, 7

## Note to Parents and Teachers

The Construction Zone set supports national science standards related to understanding
science and technology. This book describes and illustrates demolition of buildings. The
images support early readers in understanding the text. The repetition of words and
phrases helps early readers learn new words. This book also introduces early readers
to subject-specific vocabulary words, which are defined in the Glossary section. Early
readers may need assistance to read some words and to use the Table of Contents,
Glossary, Read More, Internet Sites, and Index sections of the book.

# Table of Contents

# Getting Ready

It's demolition time!
Sometimes old buildings
are torn down to make room
for new buildings.

Workers make sure

the areas are safe.

Fences and signs tell people

to stay away.

**DANGER**

**CONSTRUCTION AREA KEEP OUT**

Workers take out parts
of the buildings to use again.
They take out sinks, doors,
and windows.

# Demolition

Short buildings are smashed
with wrecking balls.
The heavy ball knocks holes
in the walls.

Loaders also ram the walls.

Excavators pull down
the pieces.

Tall buildings are demolished
with dynamite.
The buildings crumble
when the dynamite explodes.

# Cleaning Up

Loaders pick up
the piles of rubble.

Dump trucks take away
the rubble.

Bulldozers clear
and flatten the land
where the buildings stood.

# New Buildings

Soon new buildings
will be built
in the empty spaces.

# Glossary

bulldozer — a powerful tractor with a wide blade at the front; bulldozers move earth, rocks, and rubble.

dynamite — a powerful explosive

dump truck — a large truck with a bed on the back that can be tipped up

excavator — a machine with an arm and a bucket at the end that a driver can move

loader — a machine with a bucket at the front

rubble — the broken bricks, stones, and other materials left behind when a building is taken down

# Read More

**Bailer, Darice.** *Demolish.* Matchbox. New York: Little Simon, 2005.

**Graham, Ian.** *At a Construction Site.* Machines at Work. Laguna Hills, Calif.: QED Publishing, 2006.

**MacAulay, Kelley, and Bobbie Kalman.** *Cool Construction Vehicles.* Vehicles on the Move. New York: Crabtree, 2007.

**Woods, Bob.** *Massive Machines.* Reading Rocks! Mankato, Minn.: Child's World, 2007.

# Internet Sites

FactHound offers a safe, fun way to find Internet sites related to this book. All of the sites on FactHound have been researched by our staff.

Here's how:

1. Visit *www.facthound.com*

2. Choose your grade level.

3. Type in this book ID **1429612371** for age-appropriate sites. You may also browse subjects by clicking on letters, or by clicking on pictures and words.

4. Click on the **Fetch It** button.

**FactHound will fetch the best sites for you!**

# Index

Word Count: 118
Grade: 1
Early-Intervention Level: 18